DAYENU

or

HOW UNCLE MURRAY SAVED THE SEDER

With all my love
To my sister and brother-in-law
HELENE AND MURRAY WACHMAN
And their children
ELLIOT, RONALD, ADINA

GLOSSARY

Afikomen	A piece of matzah set aside for dessert. This matzah is hidden and found during the seder meal.
Charoset	Mixture of apples and nuts symbolizing the bricks and mortar used by the Israelite slaves.
Dayenu	"It would have been enough." Title of a popular Passover song.
Elijah	This prophet is invited to each seder as a symbol of peace.
Four Questions	Asked by the youngest as an introduction to the Passover story.
Gefilte Fish	Fish dumplings (a traditional Passover food).
Haggadah	Book containing the seder service.
Hametz	Bread and other food not permitted during Passover.
Kiddush	Prayer over wine.
Matzah	Unleavened bread.
Passover	Spring holiday celebrating the exodus from Egypt.
Seder	Passover meal at which the story of the exodus is retold.

DAYENU

or

HOW UNCLE MURRAY SAVED THE SEDER

by Rosalind Schilder

illustrations by Katherine Janus Kahn

KAR-BEN COPIES, INC.
ROCKVILLE, MD

Library of Congress Cataloging-in-Publication Data

Schilder, Rosalind.
  Dayenu.

  Summary: Deciding that a Passover seder is too much work, Uncle Murray and Aunt Helene
decide to skip some of the things they do every year. However, one thing leads to another and soon
a joyous celebration is underway.
  [1. Passover—Fiction] I. Kahn, Katherine, ill. II. Title.
PZ7.S34629Day 1988   [E]   88-1238
ISBN 0-930494-76-8

Aunt Helene finished vacuuming and collapsed on the sofa.

"I wish we could do something about Passover," she said to Uncle Murray, absent-mindedly wiping her forehead with the dust cloth.

"No matter how much work we do to get ready for the holiday, it's never enough."

"You're right," said Uncle Murray, as he dusted the cat napping on the piano. "Enough is never enough. But I have an idea. Why don't we skip some of the things we do every year?"

"Great idea!" said Aunt Helene.

"If we get rid of all the hametz, and don't buy matzah, it will be enough," said Uncle Murray.

So they scrubbed and scoured and dusted and mopped and vacuumed the house from top to bottom.

"We did a fine job," said Uncle Murray, as they searched each room with candle, feather, and spoon. "There is no hametz anywhere."

"And there is no food anywhere!" said Aunt Helene. "We have to buy some matzah."

"GOOD IDEA!" said Uncle Murray. "If we buy matzah, and no other Passover foods, it will be enough!"

So they went to the supermarket and piled their cart high with boxes and boxes of matzah.

"We'll get sick of eating nothing but matzah for eight days," said Aunt Helene as she unloaded the bags. "Maybe we should buy some other foods."

"GOOD IDEA!"

said Uncle Murray. If we buy other Passover foods, and do not invite guests to share it, it will be enough."

So they went back to the supermarket and loaded their cart with gefilte fish, apples, nuts, sponge cake, eggs, matzah meal, and macaroons.

"So much food and no one to share it!" said Aunt Helene, as she put all the packages away in her clean cupboards. "Let's invite a few guests."

"GOOD IDEA!"

said Uncle Murray. "If we invite guests and do not have a seder, it will be enough."

So Aunt Helene and Uncle Murray telephoned their nine nieces and nephews.

They prepared a big dinner. They chopped and sliced, and baked and

cooked all day long.

When all the guests had arrived and were seated around the holiday table, Aunt Helene looked at the unlit candles. And she looked at the empty Kiddush cup. "We have to light the candles," she said. "After all, it's Passover! Then we can recite the Kiddush."

"GOOD IDEA!" said Uncle Murray. "If we start the seder, and do not ask the Four Questions, it will be enough."

So Aunt Helene lit the holiday candles, and everyone sang the Kiddush. Then Uncle Murray began to read from the Haggadah.

When they came to the Four Questions, they stopped.

"We have to ask them," said Adina. "I've been practicing all week!"

"GOOD IDEA!" said Uncle Murray. "If we ask the Four Questions, and do not tell the story of the Exodus, it will be enough."

So Adina got up and sang:

Why is this night different from all other nights?
On all other nights we eat either bread or matzah.
  Tonight, only matzah.
On all other nights we eat all kinds of vegetables.
  Tonight, only bitter herbs.
On all other nights we do not have to dip foods even once.
  Tonight, we dip twice.
On all other nights, we eat sitting any way we like.
  Tonight, we recline.

When she finished the Four Questions, no one said a word.

"We have to tell the story," said Elliot.

"So we can find out the answers," added Jill.

"GOOD IDEA!" said Uncle Murray. "If we tell the story, and do not taste the bitter herbs, it will be enough."

So they began to read:

"Once we were slaves

and now we are free..."

But when they came to the part about the bitter life under Pharaoh's rule, they stopped again.

"We have to taste the bitter herbs, and the matzah and charoset," said Lenore, "to remind us of our life as slaves in Egypt."

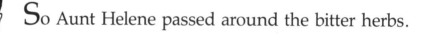 "GOOD IDEA!" said Uncle Murray. "If we taste the special foods, and do not eat the seder meal, it will be enough."

So Aunt Helene passed around the bitter herbs.

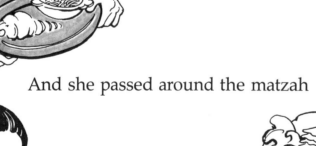

And she passed around the matzah

and charoset.

And everyone said the blessings and had a taste.

Then it was time for the seder meal.

"We have to eat it," said Jonah. "Aunt Helene and Uncle Murray worked so hard to prepare it."

"GOOD IDEA!" said Uncle Murray. "If we eat the meal and do not share the Afikomen, it will be enough."

Everyone was so hungry that the delicious food quickly disappeared.

When it was time for dessert, Lori and Judith proudly came forward with the Afikomen. "We have to eat it," they said, "because we found it."

"GOOD IDEA!" said Uncle Murray. If we share the Afikomen and do not welcome Elijah, it will be enough."

So Uncle Murray traded the Afikomen for two small gifts, and everyone ate a piece of the matzah.

Now it was time to welcome Elijah the prophet.

"We have to open the door," said Lori. "I think I hear him."

"GOOD IDEA!"   said Uncle Murray. "If we greet Elijah and do not sing the seder songs, it will be enough."

So Larry filled Elijah's cup, and Lori opened the door. Everyone watched to see if any of the wine disappeared.

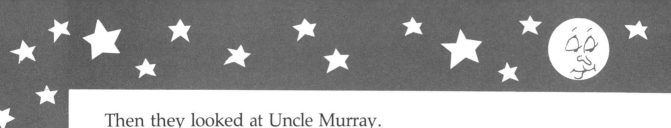

Then they looked at Uncle Murray.

"We have to sing the songs," said Ronald. "What's a seder without songs?"

"GOOD IDEA!" said Uncle Murray. "If we sing the songs, and do not finish the seder…"

"IT WILL NOT BE ENOUGH," everyone shouted.

We cleaned our house of hametz; bought matzah and Passover foods; invited guests; asked the Four Questions; told the story of the Exodus; tasted the bitter herbs, matzah, and charoset; ate the meal; shared the Afikomen; welcomed Elijah…

"So why not sing the songs
and finish the seder,"

concluded Uncle Murray.

AND THEY DID!